Welcome to The Giggle Club

The Giggle Club is a collection of picture books made to put a giggle into early reading. There are funny stories about a contrary mouse, a dancing fox, a turtle with a trumpet, a pig with a ball, a hungry monster, a laughing lobster, an elephant who sneezes away the jungle and lots more! Each of these characters is a member of **The Giggle Club**, but anyone can join: just pick up a **Giggle Club** book, read it and get giggling!

Turn to the checklist on the inside back cover and tick off the Giggle Club books you have read.

TEE HEE!

HA HA!

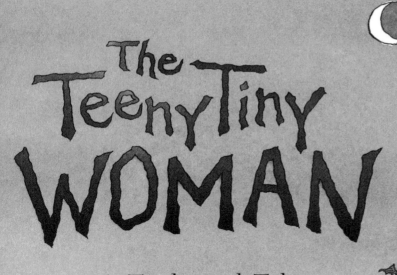

The Teeny Tiny WOMAN

A Traditional Tale

illustrated by

Arthur Robins

WALKER BOOKS
AND SUBSIDIARIES
LONDON · BOSTON · SYDNEY

Once upon a time

a teeny tiny woman

who lived in a teeny tiny house

put on her teeny tiny hat

and went out for a teeny tiny walk.

When the teeny tiny woman

had gone a teeny tiny way,

she went through a teeny tiny gate

into a teeny tiny churchyard.

In the teeny tiny churchyard

the teeny tiny woman

found a teeny tiny bone

on a teeny tiny grave.

Then the teeny tiny woman

said to her teeny tiny self,

"This teeny tiny bone

will make some teeny tiny soup

for my teeny tiny supper."

So the teeny tiny woman

took the teeny tiny bone

back to her teeny tiny house.

When she got home

she felt a teeny tiny tired,

so she put the teeny tiny bone

in her teeny tiny cupboard

and got into her teeny tiny bed

for a teeny tiny sleep.

After a teeny tiny while

the teeny tiny woman

was woken by a teeny tiny voice

that said,

"Give me my bone!"

The teeny tiny woman

was a teeny tiny frightened,

so she hid her teeny tiny head

under her teeny tiny sheet.

Then the teeny tiny voice

said a teeny tiny closer

and a teeny tiny louder,

"Give me my bone!"

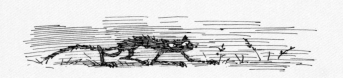

This made the teeny tiny woman

a teeny tiny more frightened,

so she hid her teeny tiny head

a teeny tiny further

under her teeny tiny sheet.

Then the teeny tiny voice

said a teeny tiny closer

and a teeny tiny louder,

"Give me my bone!"

The teeny tiny woman

was a teeny tiny more frightened,

but she put her teeny tiny head

out from under her teeny tiny sheet

and said in her loudest teeny tiny voice,

For Deirdre

First published 1998 by Walker Books Ltd
87 Vauxhall Walk, London SE11 5HJ

10 9 8 7 6 5 4 3 2 1

Text © 1998 Walker Books Ltd
Illustrations © 1998 Arthur Robins

This book has been typeset in M Perpetua

Printed in Hong Kong

British Library Cataloguing in Publication Data
A catalogue record for this book is
available from the British Library.

ISBN 0-7445-6022-5